Happy Pants

Why is Mummy so sad?

Heather Gallagher

Illustrated by Liz McGrath

Wombat Books
Stories you'll want to share

Happy Pants
Written by Heather Gallagher
Illustrated by Liz McGrath
Published by Wombat Books 2014
Paperback edition 2016

PO Box 1519, Capalaba Qld 4157
www.wombatbooks.com.au

National Library of Australia Cataloguing-in-Publication entry
Author: Gallagher, Heather, author.
Title: Happy pants / Heather Gallagher, Liz McGrath (illustrator).
ISBN: 9781925139846 (paperback)
Target Audience: For primary school age.
Subjects: Mother and child--Juvenile fiction.
              Brothers and sisters--Juvenile fiction.
              Postpartum depression--Juvenile fiction.
Other Authors/Contributors:
              McGrath, Liz, illustrator
Dewey Number: A823.4

For the Ponder and PODS girls with love
  Heather Gallagher

For Fra, who showed me how…
  Liz McGrath

When Mummy wears
her happy pants

we build sandcastles,
go out for babycinos

and have lots

and lots of cuddles.

But when she comes home with baby Darcy, her happy pants stay in her wardrobe.

'Mummy's a bit blue,'
says Daddy.

I love red – fire engines, racing cars and toffee apples.
But a person can't be a colour ... can they?

Some days, Mummy stays in bed,
sleeping all day.

'Mummy, let's cuddle,' I say.
But she lies as still as the
statue in the park.

'Only babies
sleep all day,
don't they Daddy?'

'Not always,' he says.

Some days, Mummy won't eat a thing.
'Mummy, have some of my ice-cream,' I say.

But she won't even have a lick.

'Only babies are fussy eaters, aren't they Daddy?'

'Not always,' he says.

And some days, Mummy cries all day.
'Mummy, Big Ted will cheer you up,' I say.

But she just cries into his fur, until it's soggy.

'Only babies
cry all day,
don't they
Daddy?'

'Not always,'
he says.

One day
I sneak into
Mummy's wardrobe.

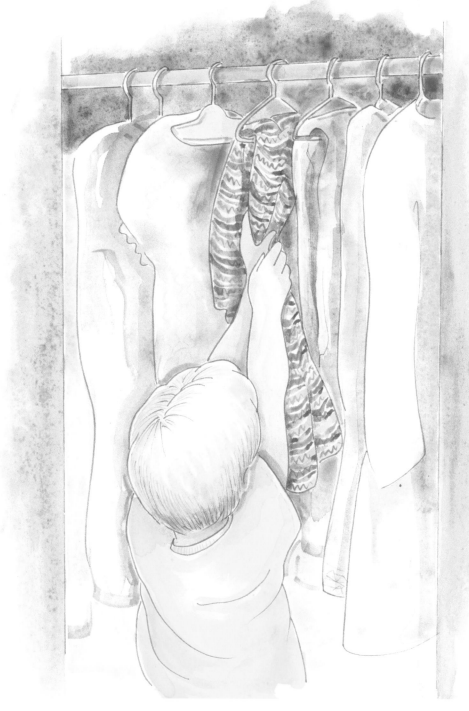

I pull Mummy's happy pants off the hanger.

As I hide the pants in the cubby, they get stuck on a nail and rip!

'Uh-Oh!'

I don't even get in trouble.

Can you put a band-aid
on your heart?

Later, Gran comes to look after us.

Daddy says
he's taking
Mummy to
the doctor.

We bake cookies
and Gran lets us
eat some dough.

While the cookies are in the oven,
Darcy and I play cubbies and
Gran mends Mummy's happy pants.

When Mummy and Daddy get home I meet them at the door. 'Did the doctor make you better Mummy?'

'Not quite, my love,' she says. 'You'll need to be patient with me … but I will get better, I promise.'

'I love you, Mummy!'

'And I love
you too,
sweet thing!'
she says.
'Always.'

Depression and anxiety during or following pregnancy is known as perinatal depression. In Australia, it affects one in seven new mothers and one in ten new fathers.

Perinatal depression can mean different things to each mother but usually includes feelings of anxiety, sadness and difficulty coping, that last for more than two weeks.

Beyond the sadness, characteristic of perinatal depression, there is recovery. With early detection, support, counselling and sometimes medication, most mothers get better and enjoy their baby and the experience of motherhood.

For further information and support contact:

PANDA (Post and Antenatal Depression Association) helpline Ph: 1300 726 306
www.panda.org.au

COPE (Centre of Perinatal Excellence)
www.cope.org.au

beyondblue Ph:1300 22 4636
www.beyondblue.org.au/the-facts/pregnancy-and-early-parenthood

Gidget Foundation
www.gidgetfoundation.com.au

Lifeline Australia Ph: 13 11 14
www.lifeline.org.au